For David, First Toymaker to the Empress —C. R.

To Katrin and my amazingly awesome daughter, Allister —M. L.

Text copyright © 2012 by Candace Ryan
Illustrations copyright © 2012 by Mike Lowery

First published in the United States of America in April 2012
by Walker Publishing Company, Inc., a division of Bloomsbury Publishing, Inc.
www.bloomsburykids.com

For information about permission to reproduce selections from this book, write to
Permissions, Walker BFYR, 175 Fifth Avenue, New York, New York 10010

Library of Congress Cataloging-in-Publication Data
Ryan, Candace.
Moo hoo / by Candace Ryan ; illustrated by Mike Lowery.
p.   cm.
Summary: Cow and Owl are best friends, but when a new Kangaroo tries to join them they must decide whether or not Roo should be included.
ISBN 978-0-8027-2336-9 (hardcover) • ISBN 978-0-8027-2337-6 (reinforced)
[1. Best friends—Fiction. 2. Friendship—Fiction. 3. Cows—Fiction. 4. Owls—Fiction. 5. Kangaroos—Fiction.] I. Lowery, Mike, ill. II. Title.
PZ7.R9477Mo 2012   [E]—dc22   2010049589

Art created with pencil, traditional screen printing, and print gocco and finished digitally
Text hand-lettered by Mike Lowery
Book design by Regina Roff

Printed in China by C&C Offset Printing Co., Ltd., Shenzhen, Guangdong
2 4 6 8 10 9 7 5 3 1 (hardcover)
2 4 6 8 10 9 7 5 3 1 (reinforced)

Candace Ryan would like to extend special thanks to
Stacy Cantor Abrams, Mike Lowery, Donna Mark, Regina Roff, and Kelly Sonnack.

MOO HOO

CANDACE RYAN

illustrated by
mike LOWERY

Walker & Company New York

COW AND OWL ARE FRIENDS.

THEY MAKE
MUSIC
TOGETHER.

MOO HOO.
TWO COO.

THEY FIX
THINGS TOGETHER.

THEY EVEN GO
TRICK-OR-TREATING
TOGETHER.

MOO
HOO.

THEY DON'T KNOW
WHAT TO DO.

MOO HOO.

WHO
YOU?

KANGAROO TRIES TO
PLAY WITH THEM.

MOO HOO.

ROO THREW.

BUT COW AND OWL PRETEND NOT TO NOTICE...

MOO HOO.

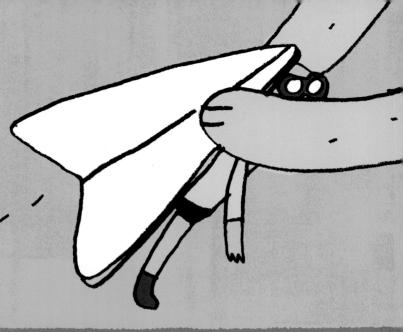

ROO TOO?

...UNTIL KANGAROO GOES AWAY.

MOO HOO.
ROO
BLUE.

BUT KANGAROO DID SEEM
KIND OF COOL.
MOO HOO.

ROO FLEW.

AND KANGAROO LIKED
WHAT THEY LIKED.

MOO
HOO.

ROO
DREW.

SO WHEN THINGS AREN'T
AS MUCH FUN ANYMORE...
MOO HOO.

BOO-
HOO.

...COW AND OWL GO ON A MISSION.

MOO HOO.

VIEW ROO?

THEY SEARCH

EVERYWHERE.

AND WHEN THEY FINALLY
FIND KANGAROO...

MOO HOO.

...THEY DISCOVER THAT THREE IS BETTER THAN TWO.

MOO HOO ROO.

NEW TRUE CREW.